Howard B. Wigglebottom Listens to a Friend

A Fable About Loss and Healing

Reverend Ana Howard Binkow

David A. Cutting

Reverend Ana Howard Binkow
Illustration: David A. Cutting
Book design: Jane Darroch Riley

Thunderbolt Publishing
We Do Listen Foundation
www.wedolisten.org

THANKS
Our special gratitude to the following people:
Andrea D'Antonio, Joanne, Sophia and Eric De Graaf, Debbi Finchum, Sherry I. Gary, Jennifer Hegerty, Beth Ivey,
Marianne Lucchesi, Cynthia Medina, Betsy Nunn, Jacqui Odell, Tori Peterson, Michelle Rhodes, Rosalie Roberts,
Julia Simpson, Karen S. Smiley, Christa Stephens, Nicohl S. Webb, Ed.S. and Rosemary Underwood

We also give appreciation and gratitude to those volunteers who gave us feedback and the schools that participated in the review process:

Bellows Spring Elementary School, Ellicott City, Maryland
Brookside School, Columbus, Ohio
Charleston Elementary School, Charleston, Arkansas
Liberty Elementary, Columbus, Ohio
Linton Elementary School, San Antonio, Texas
Monroe Elementary, St. Charles, Missouri
Mt Horeb Elementary School, Jefferson City, Tennessee
Pate's Creek Elementary School, Stockbridge, Georgia

PS 176, Brooklyn, New York
Timbercrest Elementary, Deltona, Florida
Timberwilde Elementary School, San Antonio, Texas
West Salisbury Elementary, Salisbury, Maryland
Wilson Hill School, Worthington, Ohio
Woodridge Elementary, San Antonio, Texas
Woodward Academy Primary School, College Park, Georgia

First printing: January 2015
Printed in Malaysia by Tien Wah Press (Pte) Limited.

ISBN 978-0-9910777-4-8
LCCN 2014955776

This book belongs to

_____

Howard B. Wigglebottom loved to tell knock – knock jokes to make his friends laugh.

He was very surprised though when Kiki – instead of asking him "Who's there?" – hit him with a book and ran.

Howard went after her to find out what was going on.

At the corner, he saw Buzz.

"Did Kiki do that to you?" Howard asked.

"Yes," Buzz answered, "and then she ran that way. I think she is having a bad day."

On the next block over Howard saw Poochie.

"Was it Kiki?"

"Yes," said Poochie, "and she ran that way. I think she's having a very bad day."

9

A few minutes later Howard bumped into Ali.

"Did Kiki do that too? I heard she's having a horrible day."

Ali nodded yes and pointed her finger showing Howard which way Kiki went.

Next was Oinky.

"Kiki, right?" asked Howard.

"Yes," Oinky answered, cleaning himself up. "She just ran home crying. Looks like she's having a really horrible day."

Howard was worried. "What's up with Kiki?" He asked his friends
"Any idea, anyone?

"I think her puppy died," answered Poochie.

"Oh poor Kiki. Now I understand why she was doing mean things to us.
I don't like it when things stop working or die either. It's so sad. What can we
do to help her feel better?" Howard wondered. "Maybe a show and tell about
her puppy?"

"Show and tells are nice to help us feel better when a loved one dies," said Ali, "but what if Kiki doesn't want that now?

Maybe she will feel better if we help her count her blessings, you know, keep talking about all the good and fun stuff she does have in her life?"

"Telling her how lucky she is to make her feel better is a good idea, but what if Kiki doesn't want that now?" said Poochie.
"Maybe she will feel better if she does nice things for her family and friends."

"Helping others does help us feel better after a loved one dies, but what if Kiki doesn't want that right now?" said Buzz.

"I think she needs to scream like crazy many times, kick a bunch of pillows, and punch sand bags as hard as she can to really feel better."

21

"Nah," said Oinky. "Your ideas are all good but not for Kiki right now. I think she will feel better if we ask her to come out and play a wild soccer game with us."

"All these ideas are good and helpful," Howard said, "but we need to ask HER what she feels like doing. Who is brave enough to go in her room? Let's draw straws. The one who draws the shortest will go talk to Kiki."

Howard got the short one.

"Are you scared she's going to beat you up?" asked Ali? "I would…"

"I will go prepared," Howard answered.

After Howard got ready, they all went to Kiki's house and slowly opened the door to her room.

"Kiki," Howard said, "I have a quick question then I'll go away. What will make you feel better about your puppy dying?"

Kiki took a while to answer. "I don't know for sure. Right now I want to be quiet in my room," she said sadly.

Howard and his friends listened to her wishes and left her alone.

They made a nice card telling her they loved and missed her and were ready to help and to play whenever she was.

And that made Kiki feel much better!!

Howard B. Wigglebottom Listens to a Friend:
A Fable About Loss and Healing
Suggestions for Lessons and Reflections

LIFE'S RULES

We may not like it, but just like in school, life on this planet has many rules. Here are some of life's rules: there are days with light and nights with darkness, if things go up they must come down (except rocket ships going into outer space), things will not happen the way we want all the time, things are not always fair, everyone will experience pain of some kind, everything changes and ends, and all people and pets will die someday.

WHEN THEY BREAK, STOP WORKING, OR DIE

It's very sad when things, pets, and people we love break, stop working, or die. It's a part of life we don't even like to talk about.

When we do talk about it though, we get to feel better. What does it mean to die?

When people or pets die, their bodies stop working. They can't walk, play, speak, eat, see, hear, sleep, feel pain, or feel good. We don't get to be with them anymore.

Does everyone die? Yes, everyone will die. It's one of life's rules. We feel very sad when it happens and we will have many bad days, but with time we all will feel better.

FEELING SAD OR MAD?

When a loved one dies, we may get very sad or mad and have very bad days like Kiki did, or we may want to stay quiet and alone for some time. Some of us may want to cry a lot, or we may want to play and run just like nothing happened. Whatever we may feel like doing or saying is OK, as long as we apologize to people in case we do or say something not nice.

It might take many days to feel better again, and even then, the sadness will be on and off for a long time until it is more off than on.

THINGS TO DO TO FEEL BETTER

While we wait for the sadness to lift, there are a few things we can do to feel better when a loved one dies:

- have a show and tell about the person or pet

- play outdoor games like soccer or football, or jump rope or climb stairs very fast

- kick, scream, and punch pillows or punching bags

-count your blessings

-volunteer to help your parents, neighbors, young children, or a teacher

- sit next to a window, a tree, or a pond and watch the clouds go by

-watch your favorite movie over and over

-read your favorite book

-draw pictures

When we are trying to help a friend or relative whose loved one died,we need to be very patient and forgiving. Just like Kiki our friend or relative may be mean, strange, no fun and may not want to see or talk to us for a while. If the friend or relative say "I want to be alone" we must leave them alone until they are ready to come out and play with us again. Remember to be loving and patient!

BOOKS IN THE SERIES

WEB SITE

Visit www.wedolisten.org:
• Enjoy free animated books, games, and songs.
• Print lessons and posters from the books, and contact us.